Thumbelina

Published by Magna Books
Magna Road
Wigston
Leicester LE18 4ZH

© 1994 Twin Books Ltd

Produced by
TWIN BOOKS
Kimbolton House
117A Fulham Road
London SW3 6RL
England

Directed by CND – Muriel Nathan-Deiller
Illustrated by Van Gool – Lefèvre – Loiseaux
Text adapted by Marian Jones

ISBN: 1-85422-678-9

Printed in Slovenia

"'VAN GOOL'S'"

Thumbelina

MAGNA BOOKS

Once there was a woman who was sad because she had no children. She went to see a witch and said, "Please help me. I would like so much to have a little girl."

In exchange for a few coins the witch gave her a small seed. As soon as the woman got home she planted it in a pot. Then she went to bed.

What a surprise she had the next morning: a magnificent tulip had grown overnight! The woman was delighted and gently kissed the flower. As her lips touched the silky petals . . .

. . . they opened, revealing a little girl inside! She was delicate, and no bigger than the woman's thumb.

"I'll call you Thumbelina," the woman said.

That evening she put Thumbelina to
bed in a nutshell, giving her a rose petal
as a blanket.

The next day the woman made Thumbelina a boat by floating a leaf in a plate of water. Thumbelina was so happy she began to sing. She sang for hours. Her lovely, pure voice could be heard throughout the surrounding countryside.

Unfortunately a toad nearby heard it and thought, "That girl sings so beautifully, she must be very pretty."

In the dead of night, the toad hopped through the window and kidnapped Thumbelina as she slept in her bed.

"I've found a wife for my son," he croaked happily as he carried the girl away.

He hopped off to the marsh where his son was waiting.
"What do you think?" he asked, pointing to the sleeping
girl. "She's sweet, isn't she?"

"Very pretty," agreed the ugly son. "She will make a
delightful wife. But if she sees me, she'll run away!"

"Then let's make sure she can't get away," said the father.
He put the cradle on a waterlily leaf in the little stream
which crossed the marsh.

When Thumbelina woke up the next morning she nearly fell into the water as she got out of bed.

"Where am I?" she cried.

"You're with us now," said the father toad, "and you're most welcome."

"But I don't know you!" said Thumbelina. "I want my mother! I want to go home!"

"This is your home from now on," replied the toad. "And this is your future husband." He pointed to his son, the ugly toad!

"The wedding will be tomorrow," he said. "There's no time to lose. We must go and get ready for the ceremony." The toads hopped away.

Poor Thumbelina, who couldn't escape without falling into the water, was so upset that she burst into tears.

It happened that some fish in the stream had heard all this. They rushed to help Thumbelina. Really, they thought, she couldn't possibly marry that awful toad! *Snap!* They bit quickly through the stalk that held the waterlily, so that the leaf floated downstream.

Away went Thumbelina, far beyond where the toads could reach her. Some birds watched the little girl gliding along the water and chirped happily, "What a delightful little person! How nice she looks! How sweet she is!" They would have liked to stop her to have a closer look, but a maybug got there first!

He landed by Thumbelina, caught
gently hold of her and carried her up into
a tree.

"Don't be afraid," he said. "I just want to introduce you to my family." But when the young lady maybugs saw Thumbelina, they hissed like jealous cats.

"Look," they said, "she has only two legs! She's got no wings at all! Goodness, isn't she ugly!"

The maybug had thought Thumbelina was beautiful, but he began to believe the others when they said she was ugly. He took the girl from the tree and set her on a daisy.

As soon as Thumbelina
was alone she made a
hammock out of little
pieces of straw. She chose
a leaf to be her sunshade
and fixed the hammock
under it. It was a lovely
house! She was thirsty and
hungry, so she sipped a
drop of dew and sucked
the nectar from a flower.
Then she felt better.

Thumbelina liked living in the forest. She had rainwater to drink, berries to eat, and the birds for company.

Sadly, one day, the birds flew away. The leaf which sheltered her fell off the tree and a cold wind blew. Autumn had arrived.

Suddenly everything had changed. There was no sweet grass to lie on, no joyful birdsong in the branches, and nothing left to eat. But it was even worse when winter arrived, bringing snow and frosts.

Thumbelina was cold and unhappy.

Thumbelina decided to leave the forest. Her feet were freezing, but she walked miles through cornfields, tearing her clothes on the stubble. Finally she found a tiny house. She knocked on the door to ask for something to eat. A field mouse opened the door and kindly invited her in.

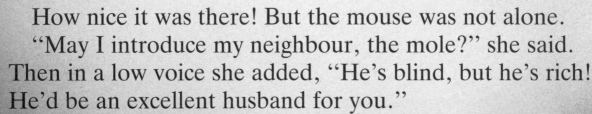

How nice it was there! But the mouse was not alone. "May I introduce my neighbour, the mole?" she said. Then in a low voice she added, "He's blind, but he's rich! He'd be an excellent husband for you."

"Why do they all want to marry me off?" wondered Thumbelina. But she shook the neighbour's fat hand anyway.

"Would you do me the honour of having a drink at my house?" he asked most gallantly. Thumbelina politely accepted. As they all walked along an underground tunnel, she bumped into a bird which lay absolutely still.

"He's sick," she cried.

"Or dead," said the mole. "Those brainless birds sing all summer long and then when winter comes they've nothing to eat. It's the same every year. Don't bother trying to help him."

Thumbelina reluctantly followed her companions. But that evening, when the others were asleep, she thought about the beautiful songbirds who had cheered her all summer with their songs. She wove a blanket of hay, and crept down the passage to the bird. She covered him with the blanket and hugged him gently.

"His heart is beating!" she whispered. "I knew it! He's just numb with cold!"

The next day she went to see the bird again. He was awake. She explained how she'd found and covered him.

"What happened to you?" she asked.

"I got lost," he said. "All my friends flew off to the warm countries. Without you I'd have died of cold!"

"I'll bring you some food every night," said Thumbelina, "and gradually you'll get better. One day you'll be able to fly away. But not before spring!"

Thumbelina was right. When spring arrived the bird was better. He decided to go and find his friends.

"Come with me," he said to the girl. "You can't spend your whole life underground! I'll carry you on my back and show you some wonderful places!"

"I'd love to," she said, "but the mouse who saved my life would be terribly unhappy. Farewell, little bird. Have a lovely journey off to the sunny countries."

When summer came Thumbelina found it very difficult to stay shut away in the dark house. She sat spinning wool and dreaming of travelling to sunny places instead of thinking of marrying the tiresome mole.

But the mouse always said, "Hurry, your wedding day is getting close. If you don't hurry up your trousseau will never be finished."

On the wedding day itself, the mole arrived in his bridegroom's suit.

"I've come for my fiancee," he said. Thumbelina took a last look out the door. "Goodbye, sun!" she whispered sadly, "I'll never see you again. Goodbye blue sky, goodbye!"

But just as she turned to come in, her
friend the bird suddenly flew down from
the sky!

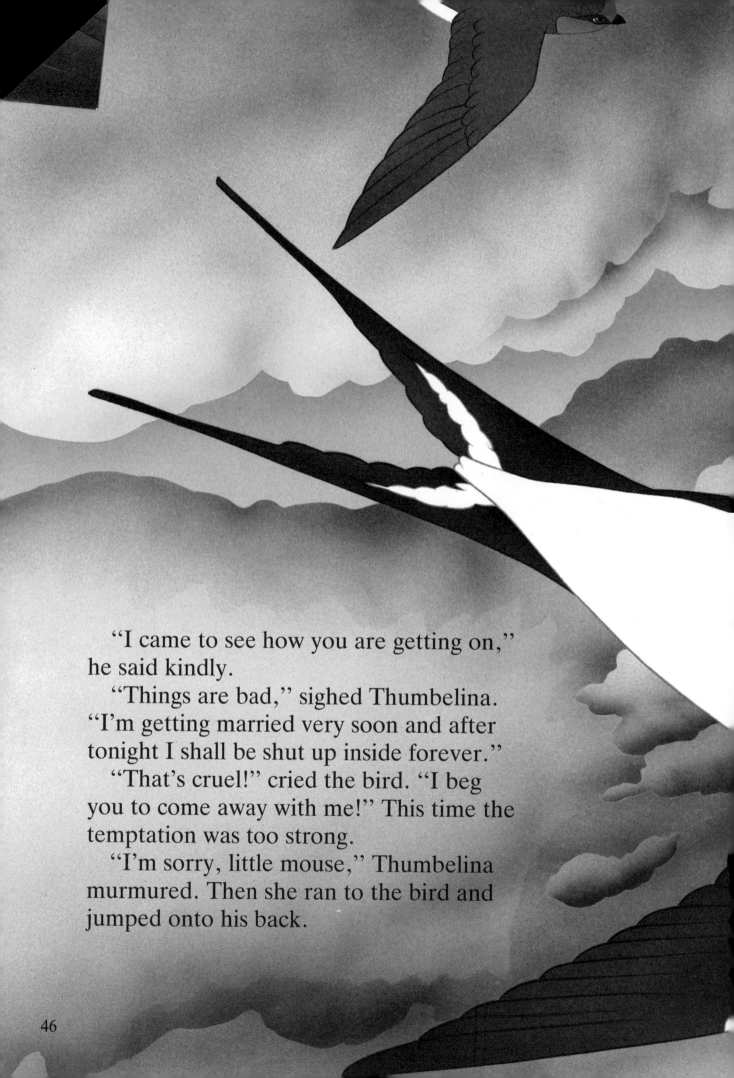

"I came to see how you are getting on," he said kindly.

"Things are bad," sighed Thumbelina. "I'm getting married very soon and after tonight I shall be shut up inside forever."

"That's cruel!" cried the bird. "I beg you to come away with me!" This time the temptation was too strong.

"I'm sorry, little mouse," Thumbelina murmured. Then she ran to the bird and jumped onto his back.

It was autumn. This time the bird was determined to fly far enough away to find a sunny country where there is no winter. What a wonderful journey they had!

They flew over mountains and across the sea and came to an enchanting country full of golden grapes, sweet-scented lemons and meadows of wild flowers. The bird alighted near a magnificent palace on a hillside.

"Choose your favourite flower," said the bird. "It will be your home."

Thumbelina stepped down and walked from one flower to another. It was very hard to choose, but finally she decided.

"This one!" she said. Then she got a surprise. There was already someone living on it.

The young man on the flower looked at
her and smiled. "Hello!" he called. He
was no bigger than Thumbelina. Not
only did he have beautiful eyes and a
splendid gold crown on his head, but
there were also two transparent wings
fluttering on his back.

"Who are you?" asked Thumbelina.

"I'm the King of the Flowers," he replied. "And you?"

"Thumbelina is my name."

The king thought she was the loveliest maiden he'd ever seen. He put his crown on her head, then leaned towards her. "Will you be my Queen?" he asked.

Thumbelina thought how different he was from the hideous toad and the blind old mole, and said, "yes."

The king kissed her.

Suddenly from each flower came a fairy.
"They're the princes and princesses of
my kingdom," said the king. "They've
come to bring us wedding presents."

Thumbelina was given all kinds of delightful gifts, but her favourite was a pair of delicate wings. They were fastened to Thumbelina's back.

"From now on you'll be able to fly like me," said the king. And together they flew off above the tulips.

And that is how Thumbelina became Queen of the Flowers. She wanted to say thank you to her friend the bird, but he'd already gone. He travelled the world, stopping to tell his story wherever he found people with loving hearts who would listen to the tale and understand it.